P9-CCZ-132

LITTLE TUG

TUG

STEPHEN SAVAGE

A NEAL PORTER BOOK
ROARING BROOK PRESS
NEW YORK

Copyright © 2012 by Stephen Savage
A Neal Porter Book
Published by Roaring Brook Press
Roaring Brook Press is a division of Holtzbrinck Publishing Holdings Limited Partnership
175 Fifth Avenue, New York, New York 10010
mackids.com
All rights reserved

Library of Congress Cataloging-in-Publication Data

Savage, Stephen, 1965-
    Little Tug / Stephen Savage. — 1st ed.
       p. cm.
    Summary: Little Tug knows what to do when the tall ship, the speedboat,
and the ocean liner need him, and at such times, he is indispensible.
    ISBN 978-1-59643-648-0 (alk. paper)
    [1. Tugboats—Fiction.] I. Title.
    PZ7.S2615Li 2012
    [E]—dc23

                                                            2011033799

Roaring Brook Press books are available for special promotions and premiums.
For details contact: Director of Special Markets, Holtzbrinck Publishers.

First edition 2012
Printed in China by Toppan Leefung Printing Ltd., Dongguan City, Guangdong Province
1 3 5 7 9 8 6 4 2

R0426910099

To Michele, who loves the water

He's not the tallest boat
in the harbor.

Meet Little Tug.

He's not the fastest boat
in the harbor.

He's not the biggest boat
in the harbor.

But when the tall ship is still,

and the speedboat's motor
breaks down,

and the big ocean liner
can't fit into the harbor,

he pulls,

he pushes,

and guides the boats to safety.

What happens when
Little Tug tires out?

The tall ship tucks him in with his sail.

The speedboat hums him a lullaby with her motor.

And the great big ocean liner
gives Little Tug a great big—